RACE CARS

By Jenny Devenny, LCSW
Edited by Charnaie Gordon

Frances Lincoln
Children's Books

AUTHOR'S NOTE

Race Cars originated through my Masters in Social Work and was an attempt to answer my own questions about how to talk to kids about race, as I navigated working as a white therapist with predominantly Black children and families. Since then, I've been delighted to see readers of all ages and races using the book as a tool to jump-start discussions. I am thrilled to collaborate with Charnaie Gordon to bring out this thoughtfully updated edition.

My hope in writing *Race Cars* was to support BIPOC [Black, Indigenous and People of Colour] children in resisting social messages of racial inferiority and to support white children in developing a positive self-concept that enables them to like themselves without needing to feel superior to anyone. My goals are for children to recognise unfairness, develop the emotional empathy to know that bias hurts and to feel empowered to disrupt racism in their own lives.

Race Cars is purposefully simplistic. It is meant to be read often and as part of a library of diverse books that foster self-love and celebrate differences. The more you read this book the more you will get out of it, so don't be discouraged if your first conversations don't go as planned. Children want to know more about unfairness and how to make an unfair situation fair and will give you plenty of opportunities to try again. Thank you for taking this important first step.

– Jenny Devenny, LCSW

EDITOR'S NOTE

In recent months, discussions about racism, bias and white privilege have been at the forefront of our everyday lives. Many people avoid these discussions because they fear that conversations about these topics lead to feelings of guilt, anger, discomfort, sadness and at times disrespect. The current state of our world, however, no longer allows for these tough conversations to be ignored. That is why I decided to take this project on and edit this story in collaboration with author Jenny Devenny. I am so happy with how this story has evolved and I hope YOU as the reader will enjoy it too.

While uncomfortable for some, we are in a position to lead or at least participate in tough conversations with children. It is my hope that readers will use this book to engage in constructive dialogue about privilege, prejudice, racism and the ways that all of us can work together to shift the conversation from hate and violence toward understanding and respect, to ultimately bring about positive change and unity to our communities.

In addition, I hope white children recognise that having privilege does not require them to feel guilty for their privilege. Use this book as a conversation starter to discuss how privilege looks in our society and which groups have privilege and which do not.

As with any book, *Race Cars* is meant to help springboard conversations. It is still up to each person committed to racial justice and equality to do their part. There is still so much more work to be done, but I believe the work is worth our time, effort and energy, because our children's lives are at stake. Thank you for reading and supporting this important book.

– Charnaie Gordon

TIPS FOR READING RACE CARS WITH KIDS

Stop and think critically: When reading the story, stop at various points to give children a chance to discuss what's happening. Refer back to what you already know about the characters and encourage children to make predictions based on this information. For example: *"We know that Chase is a black car and that the organisers of the race want a white car to win. What do you think they might do to make sure he doesn't win? Is that fair?"*

Reach for feelings and activate children's moral imaginations: Have children consider what the characters in the book might be feeling as they read the story. *"Can you imagine what Chase must be feeling in this moment? Has anyone else ever felt like that?"* Encourage them to think about what they would do in that situation. *"If you noticed something unfair happening, what could you do? Where could you find help?"*

Invite full participation: When discussing difficult topics such as race, some children may tend to shut down, whereas others may dominate the conversation. Pay attention to non-verbal cues such as body language or facial expressions to get a better sense of how children are reacting to the story, in order to create space for reactions and voices that might go otherwise unnoticed.

Relate it to the wider world: *Race Cars* is a fictional book, but the book is a reflection of the wider world. Formula 1, the world's most famous race-car championship, is one of the most expensive sports to participate in, which explains why most Formula 1 drivers are white and come from rich families. In 2007, Lewis Hamilton became the first (and still only) Black driver in Formula 1 history. Overcoming racist treatment throughout his career, he has gone on to become the most successful driver in the sport. Lewis is unique, not only because he is Black but because he also comes from a working class background. Lewis is fighting to become more involved with Formula 1's governing body (similar to the committee in *Race Cars*) in order to change the rules to be more fair. Lewis is also a supporter of Black Lives Matter and anti-racism within Formula 1.

In the NASCAR Cup Series, the top racing circuit in America, Darrell "Bubba" Wallace is the only Black driver. In 2013, he became the first African-American in 50 years to win in one of NASCAR's top three national touring series. Bubba has played a critical part in NASCAR's push for inclusion and equality. In May 2020, after the killing of George Floyd by police officers in Minneapolis, Wallace spoke out about the unfair treatment of Black people by the police and called on NASCAR to ban the Confederate flag at NASCAR races. The Confederate flag, a symbol of slavery and white supremacy, was officially banned on June 10, 2020.

This is Chase.
Chase is a black race car.

This is Ace.
Ace is a white race car.

They live in a world with lots of other race cars.
Big ones, small ones, short ones, tall ones,
old ones, new ones, brown ones, blue ones.

Chase and Ace have been best friends forever.
For as long as they can remember they have been training
together for the world-famous, annual race-car race.
Last year, they were finally old enough to enter the race.

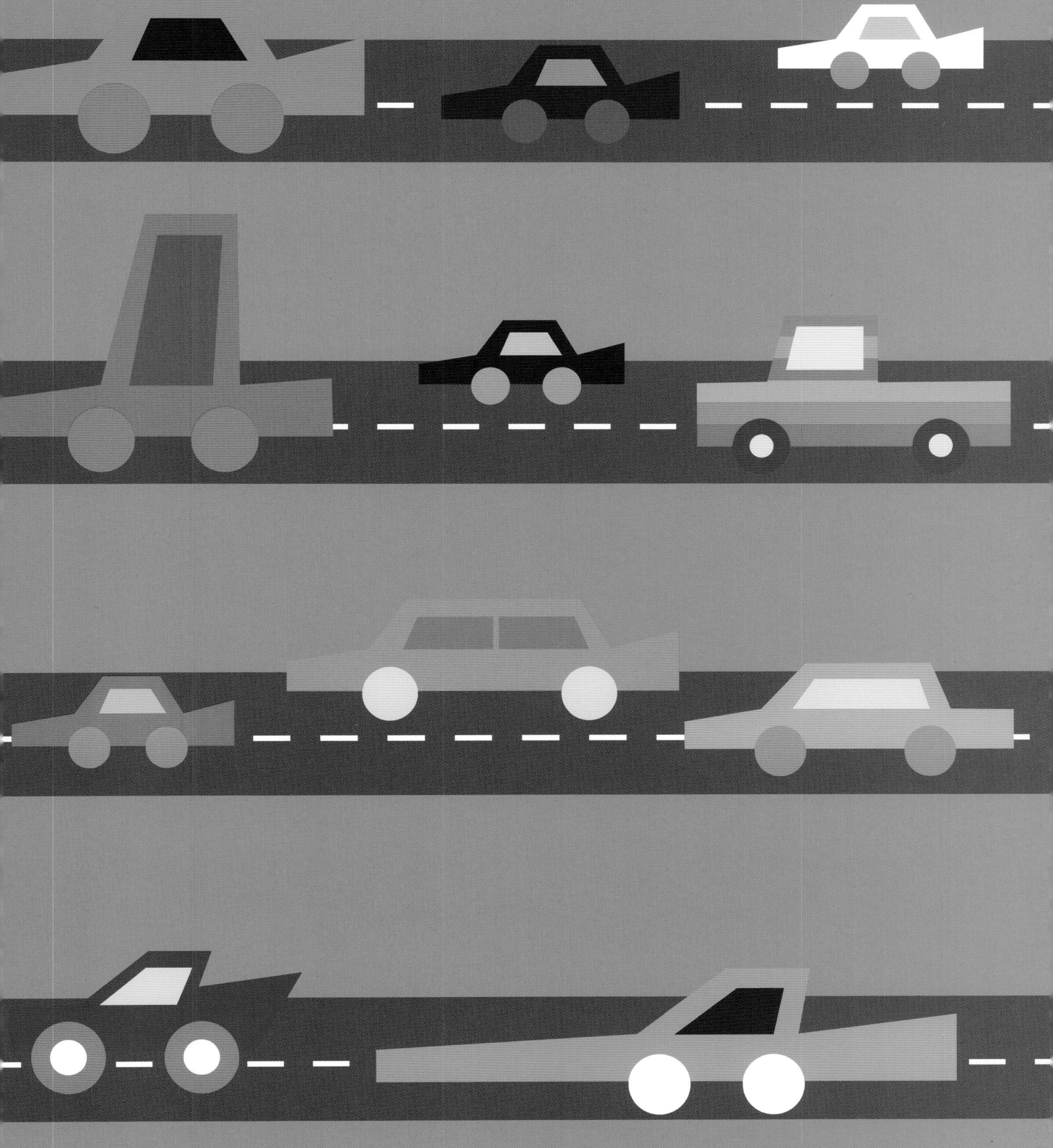

For as long as anyone could remember, every year when the big race came around, a white car would win the race. A white car would win fourth place, third place, second place and first place. Until last year…

Last year, Chase won first place and Ace won fourth place. Sometimes competition can come between friends, but not for these two. Ace was so happy for Chase and Chase was so happy for Ace. They loved to race and did not care about place.

There were, however, some cars that **did** care about place.

These cars were on the race committee.

No one had ever seen them, but everyone knew who they were. They were a group of white cars that made all the rules for the annual race-car race.

When the committee heard about Chase winning, they were not happy. A black car had **never** won first place. They did not want things to change.

"We have always given white cars the fastest tires and the most powerful engines!" they roared. "How could a black car have won?"

For the next race, the committee decided to change a few of the rules to make it easier for the white cars to win and harder for all the other cars.

They all agreed except for one... Grace. Something about it didn't feel right to her. She was used to things not feeling fair – after all, Grace was the youngest committee member and the only girl! But she didn't say anything because everyone else felt so strongly.

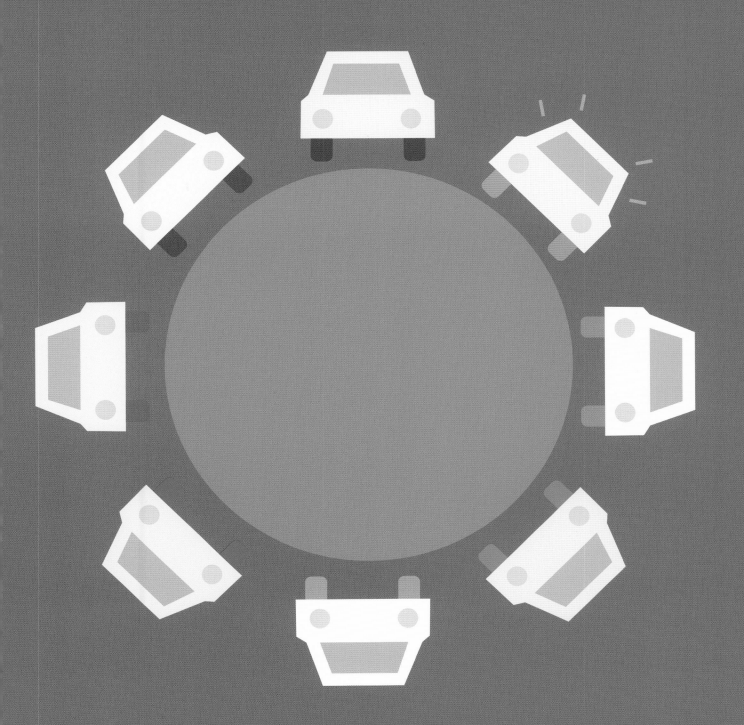

Next year rolled around and Chase and Ace were ready to race again. They had spent all summer training and knew the route by heart.

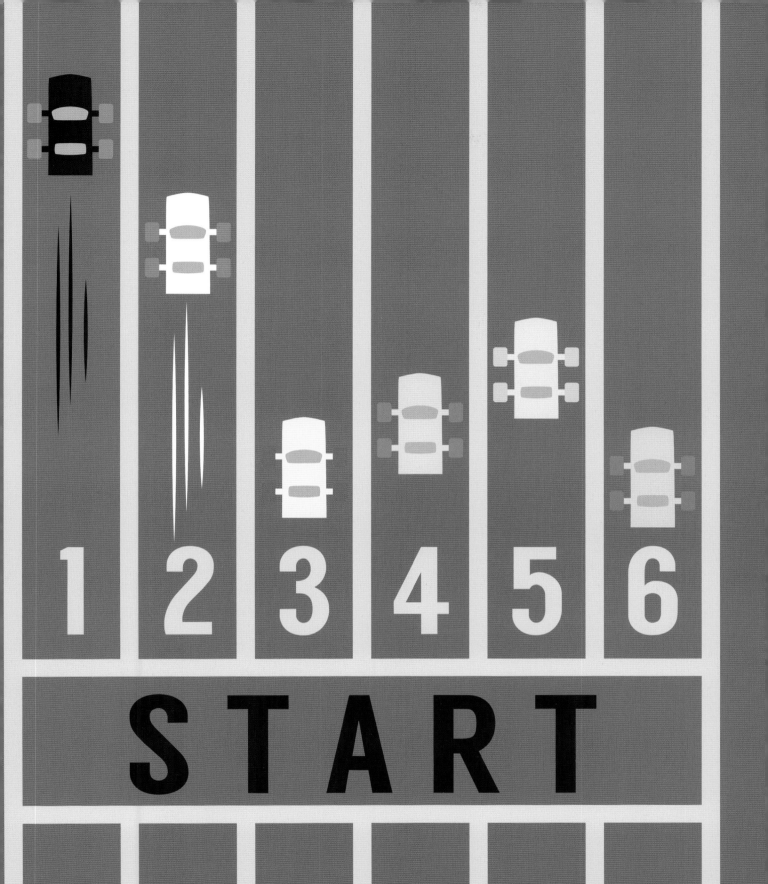

1 2 3 4 5 6

START

Chase started off faster than ever. He zipped around the track as the crowds cheered him on.

Once around the track.

Straight through the cornfield.

Over blue mountain.

Through the magical forest.

Chase was getting ready to cross the bridge when he noticed a sign that had not been there before.

"Bridge is for white cars only. All other cars must go around the river." Chase paused for a second. "Hmm…that's strange," he thought, but he did not want to waste any more time.

Chase sped around the river as fast as he could and jumped over the finish line.

Even without taking the bridge, Chase managed to come in second place. Ace came in first place. Ace was so happy for Chase and Chase was so happy for Ace. They loved to race and did not care about place.

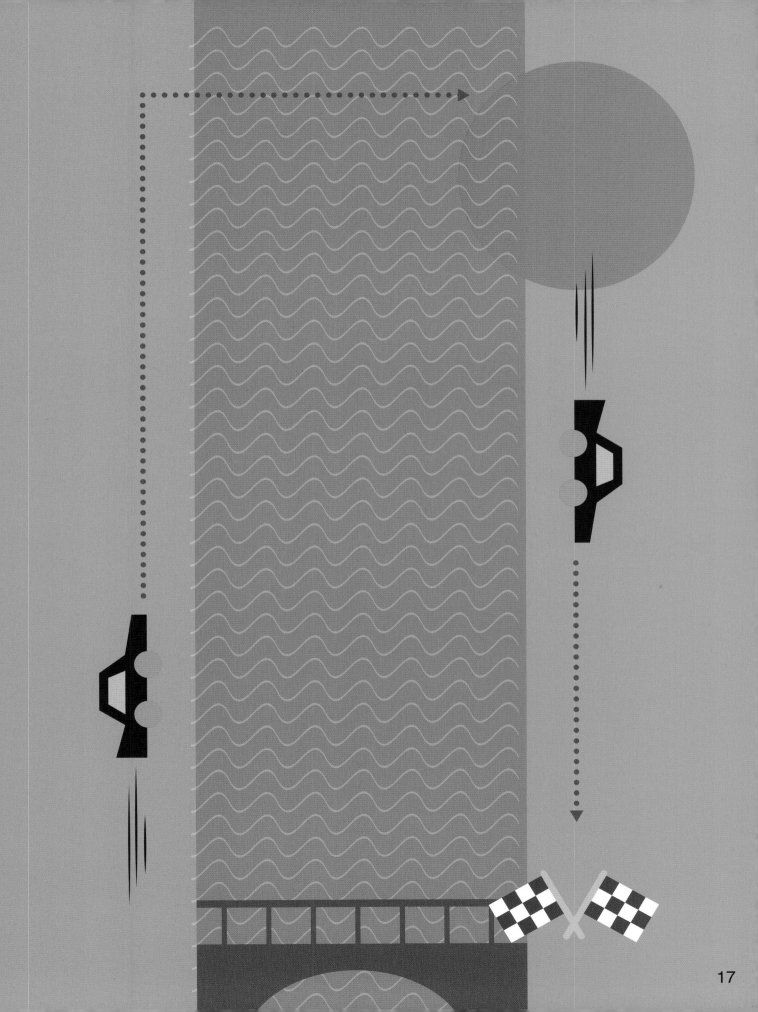

But back at home, something was bothering Chase. It just did not seem fair that the bridge was for white cars only. Was he not as good as the white cars? Was something wrong with him? He shrugged it off and decided to train even harder for next year.

Back at Ace's house, Ace was snuggled up in bed smiling. He did not expect to be faster than Chase – in their practices Chase was always fastest. "I must be getting much faster," thought Ace. He drifted off to sleep dreaming of next year's race-car race.

And back at the committee, the white cars were still not happy that Chase had won second place. They decided to change more rules to make it even easier for the white cars to win – and even harder for all other cars to win. Grace didn't think it was fair, but she didn't want to lose her place at the table, so she stayed silent.

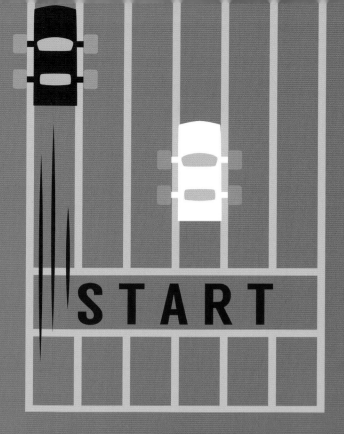

START

He zipped around the track as the crowds cheered him on.

The next year rolled around and Chase and Ace were ready to race.

Chase started off faster than ever.

He made it to blue mountain in the blink of an eye.

Then he whizzed through the cornfields in record time.

But at the top of the mountain a race officer stopped him.

"Pull over please, I need to see some identification."

Chase paused for a second. "Hmm…that's strange," he thought, "none of the white cars seem to be getting stopped," but he did not want to waste any more time. He showed the officer his identification and continued the race through the magical forest.

Chase sped around the river as fast as he could and jumped over the finish line.

But because the race officer stopped him, Chase did not place and Ace came in first instead.

Chase was happy for Ace, but they were both upset about Chase's race. They loved to race and did not care about place, but the committee had just announced a new rule. Cars that did not place this year could no longer race next year...

Next year Chase **would not** be allowed to race.

Back at home, Chase was devastated. He did not care about place, but he loved to race – what would he do now? Chase could not help feeling like he was not as good as the other cars – he felt like something was **definitely** wrong with him. Why else would he not be allowed to race? That night, Chase cried himself into a long, deep sleep.

Back at Ace's house, Ace was snuggled up in bed, but something did not feel quite right. He did not understand why Chase did not place. "He is the fastest car I know!" thought Ace.

Next year would not be the same without his best friend. Chase was the reason that Ace liked to race in the first place! Ace sighed, shrugged his shoulders and drifted off into a long, deep sleep.

Back at the building where the race committee held their meetings, Grace tried to speak out against Chase being pulled over in the race. She knew it wasn't fair and some of the members agreed, but others didn't.

"We need to change the rules of this race to make it fair and equal for all!" said Grace, softly.

"Yes, we agree!" whispered two more cars. But most remained silent and ignored her. They were afraid of change and did not want to lose their space at the table.

START

He zipped around the track as the crowds cheered him on.

Next year rolled around and Chase was at the race to cheer his best friend on.

Ace started off faster than ever.

He made it up blue mountain
in the blink of an eye.

Then he whizzed through
the cornfields in record time.

Ace was heading for the magical forest when something made him pause. A forked road with two separate paths – one for white cars and another for all other cars. "Why have I never noticed this before?" thought Ace.

Ace wanted to know what was down the other path. He wanted to understand what the race was like for Chase.

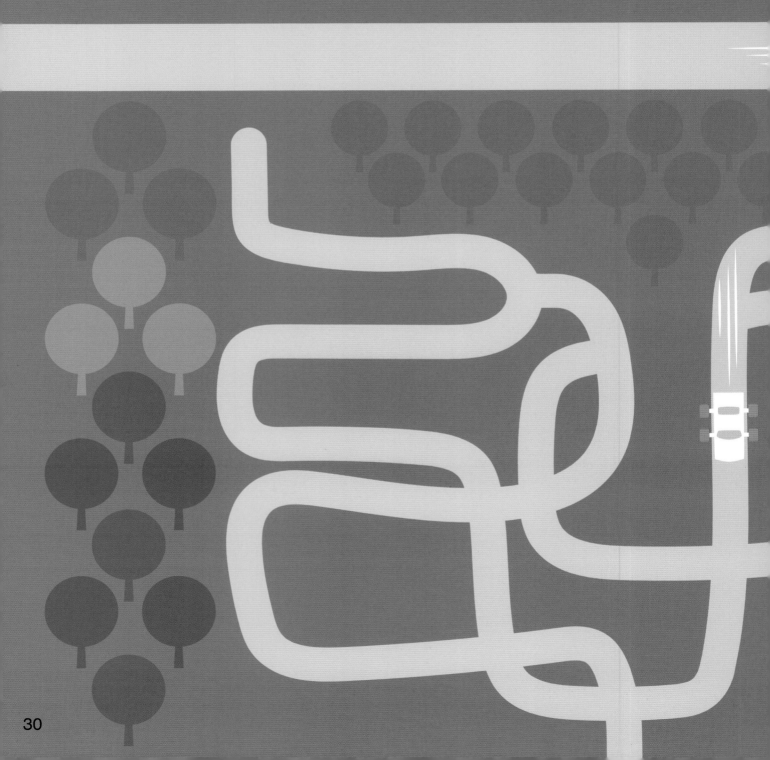

Ace took a right and went down the longer path instead of the shorter one. He sped off into the magical forest, faster and faster until he realised that he was lost.

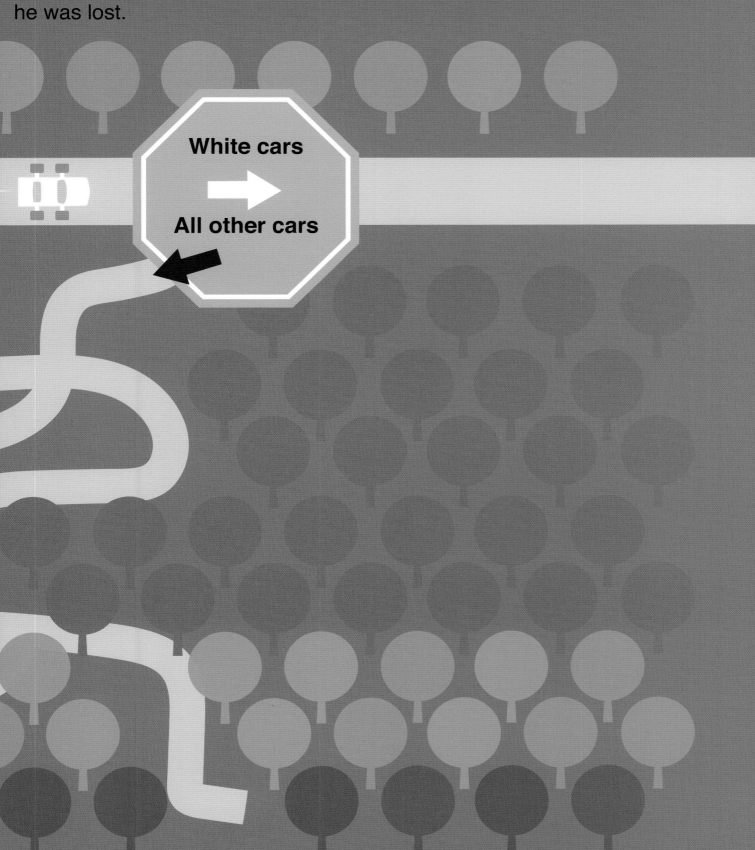

Back at the track, the race committee was starting to get worried.

All the cars had finished the race except for their star race car, Ace. Where could he be? The race officers looked everywhere but could not find Ace.

The committee decided to hold a meeting to figure out the best way to find Ace. "We need the fastest race car," said one. "The fastest race car should surely be able to find Ace."

"But Ace **is** our fastest car," said another.

"**NO!**" shouted a voice from the back of the room. The committee turned to see where it had come from. It was Grace and she could not stay silent anymore. This time they would listen.

"The fastest race car is Chase, even though we did not ever let Chase have a fair race," said Grace. "Take down those unfair signs! If we let Chase race at his fastest pace, he will definitely be able to find Ace!"

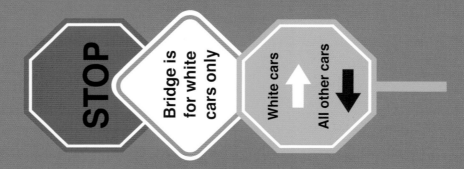

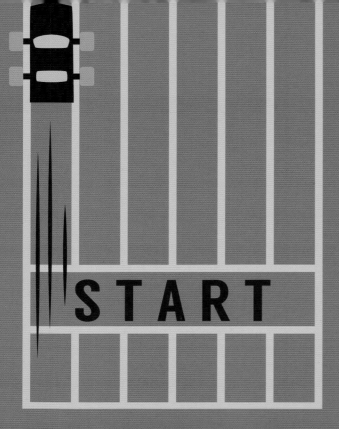

START

He zipped around the track as the crowds cheered him on.

Although Chase was still upset that the committee did not allow him to race this year, he quickly agreed to help save his best friend.

"Here I come, Ace!" said Chase.

He made it up blue mountain
in the blink of an eye.

Then he whizzed through
the cornfields in record time.

When he got to the magical forest he saw Ace speeding towards him.

"I'm sorry it took me so long to realise how much harder it was for you to win this race, Chase," said Ace.

The best friends **embraced**!